Caillou®

Plants a Tree

Adaptation of the animated series: Sarah Margaret Johanson
Illustrations taken from the animated series and adapted by Eric Sévigny

 chouette

 COOKIE JAR

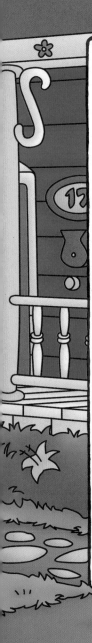

Caillou and Rosie were having fun playing in the living room. Caillou looked outside and saw his daddy. He was cutting down their maple tree.

"Mommy, what's Daddy doing to our tree?" he asked.

"Daddy and Mr. McFarlane are cutting it down," Mommy explained.

"Cutting it down? But I like that tree!" Caillou cried.

"I like it too, Caillou, but remember our tree was damaged when it was struck by lightning?" Mommy said. "It needs to be taken down."

Caillou nodded. He did remember. The thunder had been very loud, and the lightning had made the sky very bright.

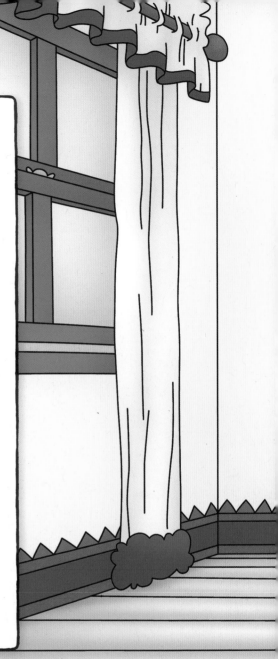

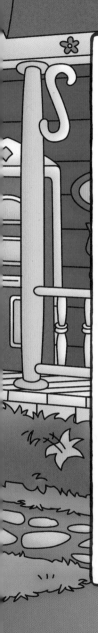

Caillou and Rosie watched as Mr. McFarlane cut down the main tree trunk. The tree fell safely to the ground, and Rosie clapped her hands.

Afterwards, Daddy came in and took off his work gloves.

"Whew, that was good exercise! Why the long face, Caillou?" he asked.

"Caillou is feeling a little sad about the old tree," Mommy explained.

"Oh, I see. Well, I'm going somewhere special today. Why don't you come with me?" Daddy said.

Caillou liked going somewhere special with Daddy.

"We're almost there, Caillou!
The tree farm is just around the
corner," Daddy said.
Caillou looked up, surprised.
"Tree farm? There are farms for
trees?" Caillou asked.
"It's kind of like the nursery where
Mommy buys her plants," Daddy
explained. "Only they grow all
kinds of trees there."

"Are we getting a new tree, Daddy?" Caillou asked.

"We sure are," Daddy replied.

"We want to replace the one we had to take down," Daddy said.

"Here we are."

Caillou looked around. There were big trees and little trees. There were trees of every kind and in every shape and size.

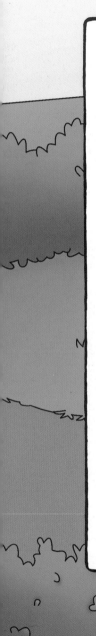

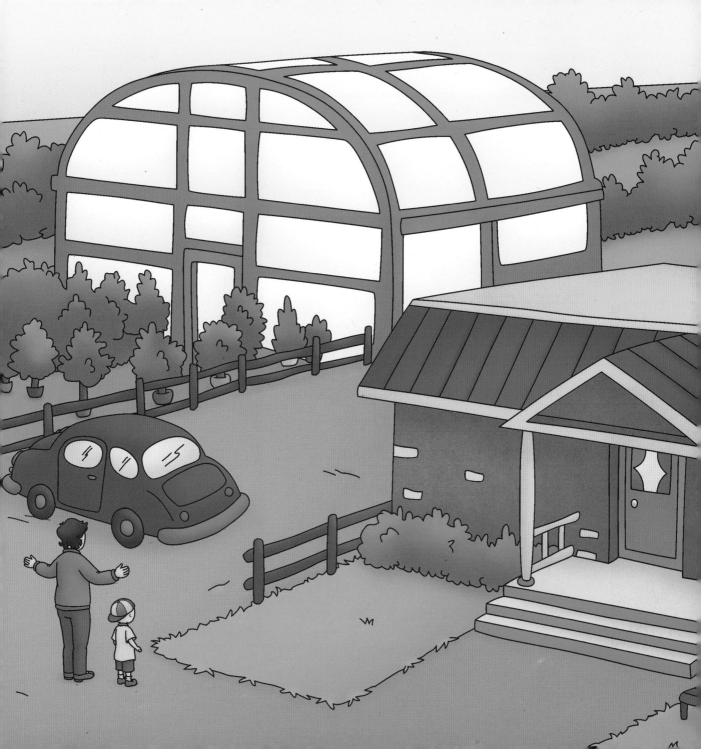

"Can I help pick out a tree, Daddy?" Caillou asked, excitedly.

"Of course. Come with me," Daddy said.

"What kind of tree are we going to get?" Caillou asked.

"One that will grow tall and give us shade over the patio in the summer for a cool place to sit," Daddy replied.

"Can we get one that the birds will like?" Caillou asked.

"Sure. Trees make great homes for birds and squirrels and other wildlife," Daddy said. "And they reduce pollution by cleaning the air that we breathe," Daddy said.

"Wow," Caillou was impressed that a tree could do all that.

Daddy and Caillou looked at
many trees, but none of them
seemed right.

Finally, Caillou saw a tree in the
distance and raced over to it.

"This one, Daddy! This is the one!"

Daddy hurried over, and he smiled
as he looked at the tree.

"A red maple. Just like our old
one. It's perfect."

When they got home, Daddy found a good spot in their yard for their new tree.

"The tree will have plenty of room to grow here," Daddy said.

"Can I help, too?" Caillou asked.

"Okay, but digging is hard work," Daddy warned.

After a little while, Caillou said, "Digging is hard work."

"It sure is, but one more shovelful and we're ready."

Mommy and Daddy finished
planting the tree. They stood back
and admired their work.
"So what do you think, Caillou?"
Daddy asked.
"I like it," Caillou cried. "Look,
the birdies like our new tree, too."
The birds and squirrels agreed:
Caillou's new tree was a
wonderful addition to the yard.

Text adapted by Sarah Margaret Johanson from the scenario of the CAILLOU animated
film series produced by Cookie Jar Entertainment Inc. (© 1997 Caillou Productions (2004) Inc.,
a subsidiary of Cookie Jar Entertainment Inc.).
All rights reserved.
Original scenario written by Sheila Dinsmore.
Original episode no 514: Caillou's Tree.
Illustrations taken from the television series CAILLOU and adapted by Eric Sévigny.
Art Direction: Monique Dupras

The PBS KIDS logo is a registered mark of PBS and is used with permission.

We acknowledge the financial support of the Government of Canada through
the Canada Book Fund for our publishing activities.

Canadian Patrimoine
Heritage canadien

We acknowledge the support of the Ministry of Culture and Communications
of Quebec and SODEC for the publication and promotion of this book.

SODEC
Québec

Bibliothèque et Archives nationales du Québec and Library
and Archives Canada cataloguing in publication

Johanson, Sarah Margaret, 1968-
Caillou plants a tree
(Ecology club)
For children aged 3 and up.

ISBN 978-2-89450-834-3

1. Ecology - Juvenile literature. 2. Tree planting - Juvenile literature. 3. Environmental protection - Juvenile
literature. I. Sévigny, Eric. II. Title. III. Series: Ecology club.

QH541.14.J63 2012   j577   C2011-942047-3

RECYCLED
Paper made from
recycled material
FSC® C10330

The use of entirely recycled
produced locally, containin
chlorine-free 100% post-co
content, saved 84 mature t

Printed in Canada
10 9 8 7 6 5 4 3 2 1   CHO1825   JAN2012